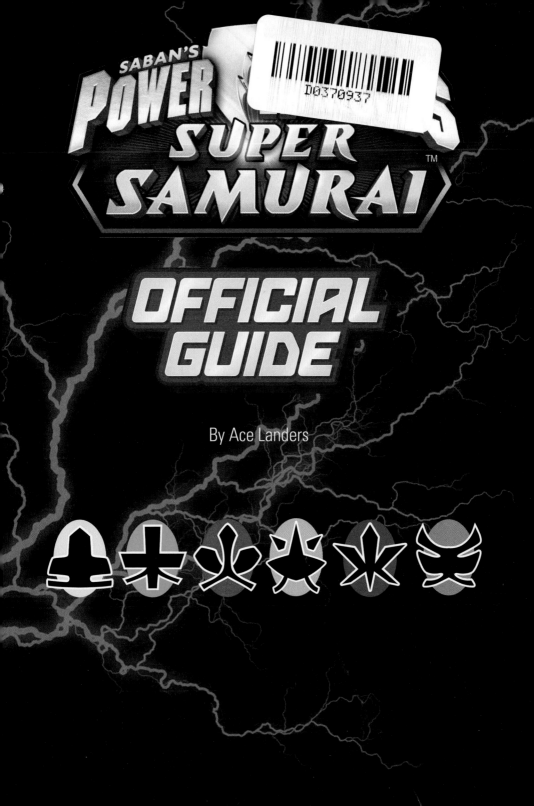

SABAN'S POWER RANGERS SUPER SAMURAI™

OFFICIAL GUIDE

By Ace Landers

SCHOLASTIC INC.

ISBN 978-0-545-44747-8

12 11 10 9 8 7 6 5 4 3 2 1   12 13 14 15 16 17/0

Printed in the U.S.A.   40
First printing, September 2012

TABLE OF CONTENTS

Centuries ago, heroic Samurai Rangers waged a war against an army of darkness. The newest generation of **Power Rangers** continue their quest to master the ancient Symbols of Samurai Power that give them control over the elements of **Fire, Water, Sky, Forest, Earth,** and **Light** in order to fend off the increasingly powerful advances of Master Xandred and his army of Nighlok.

With the guidance of their Samurai mentor, and by practicing the mysterious **Samurai Symbols of Power** and activating

the **Ancient Samurai Sword Discs**, they unlock even greater powers than previously thought possible.

POWER RANGERS
AND FRIENDS

For as long as the Nighlok have existed, there have been teams of Samurai Rangers sworn to fight them.

Led by the stoic Red Ranger, the current team of Samurai are teens who have been raised with the knowledge that one day they would be called to fight, and have inherited special powers that have been passed down through their bloodline for generations.

RED RANGER

Jayden, the Red Ranger, is the leader of the Power Rangers. He is an excellent warrior who was raised and trained by his mentor, Master Ji. Jayden is kind, caring, and fully committed to protecting our world from Master Xandred's evil plans.

FIRE SMASHER

LIONZORD

WEAPON: Spin Sword/Fire Smasher
SIGNATURE MOVE: Fire Smasher!
ELEMENT: Fire
ZORD: Lion

11

HYDRO BOW

BLUE RANGER

Kevin, the Blue Ranger, lives by the code of the Samurai. He is an extremely disciplined fighter who was raised by his father in the traditions of the Samurai. Though he wanted to be an Olympic swimmer, he put his dream on hold to join the Power Rangers Samurai.

WEAPON: Spin Sword/ Hydro Bow

SIGNATURE MOVE: Dragon Splash!

ELEMENT: Water

ZORD: Dragon

DRAGONZORD

EARTH SLICER

APEZORD

YELLOW RANGER

Emily, the Yellow Ranger, is the youngest of the Rangers. Growing up in the country, she learned to see the silver lining in everything. Her older sister was destined to be the Yellow Ranger, but Emily had to take her place when she became ill. Now nothing will stop Emily from making her sister proud.

WEAPON: Spin Sword/ Earth Slicer

SIGNATURE MOVE: Seismic Swing!

ELEMENT: Earth

ZORD: Ape

15

GREEN RANGER

Mike, the Green Ranger, is a creative rebel. He thinks outside the box and has unusual battle tactics that constantly surprise his enemies. A free spirit, Mike has a hard time fully embracing the rules of the Samurai tradition, but he is completely dedicated to the Rangers' cause.

BEARZORD

FOREST SPEAR

WEAPON: Spin Sword/ Forest Spear

SIGNATURE MOVE: Forest Vortex!

ELEMENT: Forest

ZORD: Bear

PINK RANGER

Mia, the Pink Ranger, is a confident, intuitive, and sensitive girl who cares deeply about her fellow Rangers. While she can easily blow an enemy away with her Sky Fan, Mia's dream is to one day lead a normal teenage life and find her Prince Charming.

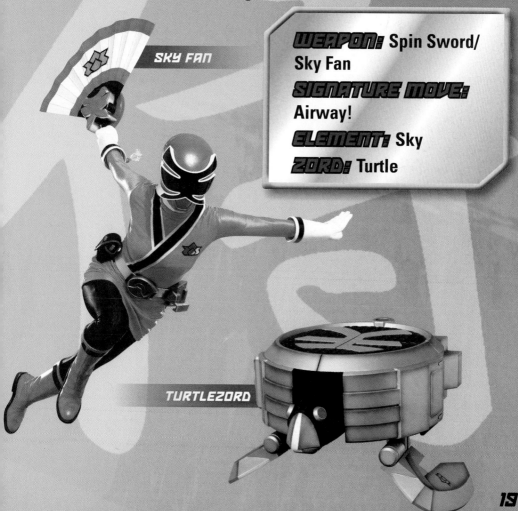

SKY FAN

WEAPON: Spin Sword/ Sky Fan
SIGNATURE MOVE: Airway!
ELEMENT: Sky
ZORD: Turtle

TURTLEZORD

19

GOLD RANGER

Antonio, the Gold Ranger, is the most outgoing and playful Samurai of the group. Unlike the others, he never received any formal Samurai training. Instead, he mastered his fighting skills on his own. This computer whiz even learned how to program his Zords by himself.

BARRACUDA BLADE

LIGHTZORD

OCTOZORD

WEAPON: Barracuda Blade
SIGNATURE MOVE: Barracuda Bite!
ELEMENT: Light
ZORD: OctoZord/LightZord

21

MENTOR JI

Mentor Ji is the guardian and authority figure to all the Rangers. He is supportive, determined, and provides guidance to the Rangers. From time to time he'll crack a joke, but he remains focused on training the Rangers to be their best!

BULK

Bulk has big dreams and fancies himself a Samurai. He wants to shape Spike into a true warrior. Unfortunately, Bulk has no idea what he's doing.

SPIKE

Spike is awkward and clumsy, but that doesn't stop him in his earnest quest to become a Samurai.

CODY

Members of Cody's family are the guardians of the first Zord that ever appeared in this world, the mighty BullZord. Infused with Symbol Power, Cody feels a connection with the Zord, and has created special discs and weapons that assist the Rangers in times of need.

NIGHLOK
AND OTHER FOES

For hundreds of years, monsters called the Nighlok have crept into our world through a gap in the fabric of time. Led by the evil Master Xandred, this army of evil creatures is out to destroy our world once and for all.

MASTER XANDRED

Master Xandred is the leader of the evil Nighlok monsters who inhabit the Netherworld. He reawakened after being shattered into a million pieces years ago, so he is not yet strong enough to travel to our dimension. Instead, he sends other Nighlok to do his dirty work. He is determined to escape his Netherworld prison by flooding the evil Sanzu River into our world with the fears and tears of those "crybaby humans."

OCTOROO

Octoroo is a small, octopus-like creature who counsels Master Xandred on the best ways to challenge and defeat the Power Rangers Samurai. He knows many things about the secrets of the Netherworld and the mythology of the Rangers contained in the ancient archives.

DAYU

Half human, half Nighlok, Dayu has survived in the Netherworld only because Master Xandred is oddly calmed by her music. The only possession she was allowed to take from the human world was her precious guitar that she loves dearly, which was transformed into the *Harmonium*.

DEKER

Even though he is half Nighlok, Deker has no interest in hurting humans. Instead, he is cursed with the desire to fight the ultimate duel. He believes the Red Ranger is his only worthy opponent, so in times of danger, he will protect the Red Ranger from other Nighlok's attacks. This angers Master Xandred greatly, but Deker cares only about his last, great battle.

MOOGERS

Moogers are malevolent creatures who squirm into our world through gaps in space and time. They are foot soldiers who exist only to serve Master Xandred. They are not very smart and are usually easily defeated. They come in giant form, too.

FURRYWORTS

Furryworts are little echo spirits that live on Xandred's ship. They annoy even the evilest Nighlok by dropping down unexpectedly and gleefully repeating everything like pesky talking parrots.

SPITFANGS

Spitfangs are frightening monsters that join the Moogers in their battles against the Rangers as Master Xandred's power increases. They spit balls of fire from their scaly crocodile-like mouths.

ROFER

Rofer has very long, strong arms that can punch through solid ground to surprise his victims from underneath them.

DOUBLETONE

Doubletone is a devious monster that tricks victims into giving up their dreams and thrives on making them cry. His special attack is the Tiger Tidal Wave, where half his body becomes a tiger while the other half becomes a tidal wave of Sanzu River water.

DREADHEAD

An incredibly strong Nighlok, Dreadhead is immune to most of the Power Ranger's weapons and is only defeated after the Red Ranger masters the powerful Beetle Disc.

NEGATRON

Negatron invades the minds of his victims to find their insecurities and then uses insults to cause them physical pain.

YAMIROR

Yamiror has dangerously stinky breath with an odor so foul that it can incapacitate anyone, even the Rangers.

MADIMOT

Madimot likes to call himself "the baddest of the bad." Armed with his shield and whip, this Nighlok's most treacherous weapon is the power of mind control.

DESPERAINO

Desperaino conjures rainstorms
that induce hopeless despair
and deepest misery in those
the rain falls upon.

ROBTISH

Robtish is a sword-wielding Nighlok with sharp fangs and a destructive focus. He rarely misses his mark, which is why Master Xandred sent him to destroy the Red Ranger.

VULPES

Vulpes is a master of spying with his powerful
interdimensional mirror called the Enchanted
Eye. The Eye also allows him to reflect back
any attack the Rangers throw his way.

STEELETO

Steeleto has a body made of razor-sharp blades that are ready to slice and dice his victims—that is, if his two giant swords don't get them first.

43

ANTBERRY

Antberry is a slippery monster that fights his adversaries by dousing them with oozy-gooey Sanzu Slime. Once slimed, the Rangers have a hard time keeping a hold of their weapons or Antberry himself.

SPLITFACE

A particularly sinister Nighlok, Splitface is made up of a series of smiling mouths that can steal the spirits of his victims.

ARACHNITOR

The Nighlok Arachnitor plots with
Octoroo to seal Master Xandred
away and take over his throne.
After he fails, Arachnitor is punished
for defying Master Xandred and
is mutated into a mindless,
powerful Nighlok.

RHINOSNORUS

With his dream mist, Rhinosnorus has the ability of putting his victims in a deep sleep and then entering their dreams. Once in this dream world, he can wolf them down at his leisure.

TOOYA

A loyal subject of Master Xandred,
Tooya attacks humans at his
master's request. He is the first Nighlok
defeated by the Power Rangers.

SCORPIONIC

Summoned by Master Xandred to scare the humans, Scorpionic uses his monstrous sword and his stinging Whirlwind Scythe Attack to terrorize and destroy everyone in sight.

SERRATOR

Serrator is a powerful Nighlok that initially pledges his allegiance to Master Xandred and vows to assist him in destroying the Samurai Rangers. However, Serrator has his own evil agenda: He wants to defeat Master Xandred and dominate the world by himself.

PAPYRUX

Massive monsters that are cut out of paper by Serrator, these giant beasts are unleashed upon the Rangers to fight his Mega Battles for him.

MUTANT ARACHNITOR

Mutated by Master Xandred as punishment for trying to defy him, the Mutant Arachnitor now survives in the human world by bathing in seeping puddles of Sanzu water.

ARMADEEVIL

Armadeevil has an ego and an apparently indestructible shell. He is sent to Earth by Master Xandred to cause havoc and misery.

SWITCHBEAST

Switchbeast can trap people's minds inside common, everyday objects, like cans or newspapers.

CRUSTOR

Under orders from Serrator to acquire the BullZord by any means necessary, Crustor shoots fireballs from his body and battles the Rangers for control of this ancient Zord.

SKARF

A gluttonous monster that serves under Serrator, this Nighlok will eat anything in sight, including the Blue Ranger's Samuraizer! Skarf's true power is revealed in his second life as a MegaMonster.

EYESCAR

Eyescar kidnaps Mentor Ji and Antonio, and uses them as bait in an attempt to lead the other Rangers into a trap.

DUPLICATOR

Duplicator has the unique talent of creating mirror images of himself, making it difficult for the Rangers to target him.

GRINOTAUR

Grinotaur rains black sand on his victims to create an insatiable hunger and thirst. Those affected never get full, and will literally eat themselves sick.

EPOXAR

Epoxar can emit globs of glue that cause his victims to stick to anything they touch, including each other!

MALDAN

Maldan leads the Nighlok into the era of the Laser Blaster, a weapon that he believes the Samurai Spin Sword is no match against. Using the Laser Blaster, he hopes to end the Power Rangers once and for all.

POWER RANGERS BATTLE MODES

In order to battle the evil Nighlok, the Rangers must utilize special powers that have been handed down to them through their Samurai family bloodlines.

The secret of a Samurai's abilities lies in their Symbol Power, which taps into the energy of the natural elements of the world. These powers can be accessed with their Samuraizers, a magical tool that the Samurai Rangers use to write Kanji symbols that unleash their awesome abilities.

SAMURAI MORPHING SEQUENCE

To begin the transformation from teens into Samurai Rangers, the Rangers first use their Samuraizers to write the Kanji symbol of their natural element and engage the Morphing Sequence.

Once the Rangers have suited up, they remove their Samurai Disc from their belts and place it on their Spin Swords, powering their weapon and completing their transformation into Samurai Rangers. They are ready for battle!

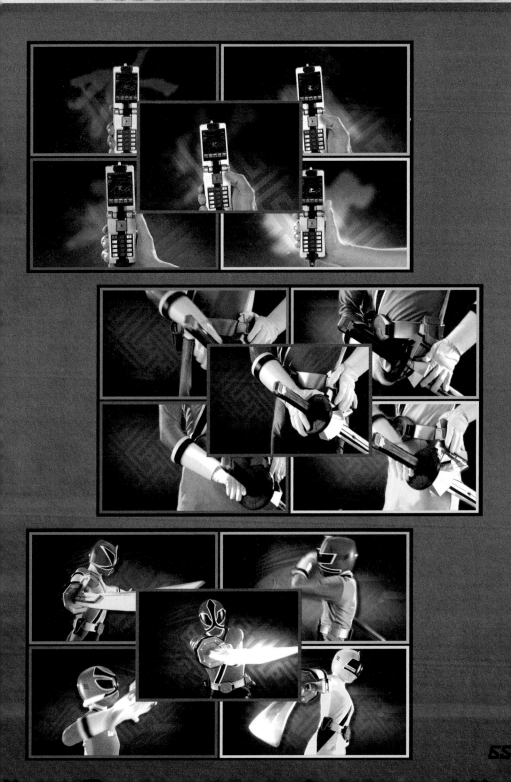

MEGA MODE MORPHING SEQUENCE

When the Rangers defeat a Nighlok, they have won only half a battle because the Nighlok have two lives. The second incarnation of a Nighlok is a giant MegaMonster who towers over the Samurai.

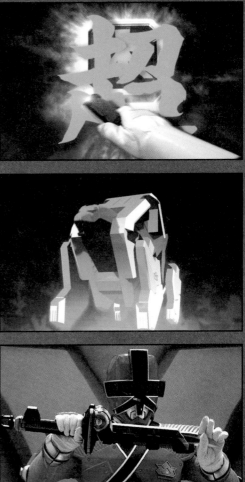

In order to battle him, each Samurai Ranger must engage Mega Mode, which enlarges their Zords into gigantic versions of themselves. The Rangers then jump into their cockpits and continue to battle at the monster's new level.

To engage Mega Mode, a Ranger begins by pulling out his Samuraizer and his FoldingZord. He writes the Kanji symbol for "large" over the Zord, which begins the transformation. The FoldingZord unfolds and grows into a giant Zord, and the Ranger morphs into his Mega Mode uniform as he jumps into the cockpit of his Zord.

SUPER SAMURAI MODE

When the Samurai Rangers finally unlock the power of the Black Box, they merge all of their Symbol Powers together and use it to become Super Samurai! Only the Ranger who uses the Black Box will receive the power-up that features a new white jacket. The Black Box then connects onto the Spin Sword and allows a single Ranger to call upon the powers of all the animal Zords.

SUPER MEGA MODE

Once in Super Samurai Mode, the Samurai Rangers can also engage Super Mega Mode inside the Megazord cockpit, which allows them to use their enhanced powers to aid in the battle against the MegaMonsters.

SHARK ATTACK MODE

With the help of the Shark Disc, the Samurai Rangers can enter Shark Attack Mode. This red jacket gives them access to the immense gifts of the Shark Sword, a powerful blade that can cause massive damage to their enemies.

SHARK ATTACK MEGA MODE

Already in Shark Attack Mode, Red Ranger can morph into Shark Attack Mega Mode, making him and his shark sword even more powerful.

SHOGUN MODE

When Jayden finally unlocks the power of the BullZord, he also unlocks Shogun Mode, the power of the ancestors, given to the Power Rangers by an apparition of the Grand Shogun.

POWER RANGERS
WEAPONS

Rangers do not fight the battle against evil without assistance. They carry with them an arsenal of weapons powered by special Power Discs. From Spin Swords to the Super Bullzooka, the Power Rangers' weapons are a force to be reckoned with for the nastiest Nighlok.

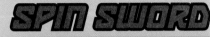

SPIN SWORD

The Spin Sword is the Power Rangers' main weapon of choice, powered by the Samurai Disc. It is upgradeable through the use of additional Power Discs, giving each Ranger the ability to morph their Spin Swords into more powerful, specialized weapons.

FIRE SMASHER

The Red Ranger's Spin Sword is upgradeable to the giant and imposing Fire Smasher, which is powered by the Red Ranger's Lion Disc.

SKY FAN

The Pink Ranger's Spin Sword morphs into the Sky Fan. When she attaches the Turtle Disc, she can control the wind.

HYDRO BOW

The Blue Ranger's Spin Sword becomes the Hydro Bow when attached to the Dragon Disc. It shoots bursts of laser arrows.

FOREST SPEAR

The Green Ranger's Spin Sword, powered by the Bear Disc, becomes the powerful Forest Spear.

EARTH SLICER

The Yellow Ranger's Spin Sword morphs into the Earth Slicer. When combined with the Ape Disc, she can fling it like an explosive boomerang.

MEGA BLADE

The Mega Blade is a large, extendable sword that the Rangers wield in their Zord and Megazord cockpits. When not extended, the Mega Blade serves as a steering device for the Zords and Megazords.

MEGAZORD'S KATANA

This giant, powerful blade materializes when the Samurai Rangers, in Mega Mode, combine their Zords into the powerful Samurai Megazord.

FIVE DISC CANNON

By combining either the Beetle, the Tiger, or the Swordfish Disc with the Fire Smasher, it upgrades to a devastatingly powerful cannon that shoots fireballs once the other Rangers load their Discs into it.

BARRACUDA BLADE

This is the Gold Ranger's version of a Spin Sword. He is able to use this weapon at such speed that it is almost invisible to the naked eye.

THE BLACK BOX

The Black Box is a magic talisman created by the very first Red Ranger. The Gold Ranger programs it in order to unite the Symbol Powers of all the Rangers into one all-powerful device.

SUPER SPIN SWORD

When the Black Box is placed on top of a Spin Sword, it becomes a Super Spin Sword. Since there is only one Black Box, only one Ranger can call on the super Black Box powers at one time.

SUPER MEGA BLADE

When the Rangers go into Super Mega Mode, they can attach the Black Box to their Mega Blade, forming the Super Mega Blade.

BULLZOOKA

Created by Cody in order to provide the Rangers with some serious laser power, the Bullzooka harnesses the Symbol Power of the BullZord using the Bullzooka Disc and turns it into a powerful laser blaster.

SUPER BULLZOOKA

When the Bullzooka is attached to the Black Box, it becomes the Super Bullzooka.

SHOGUN SPEAR

When the Bullzooka and the Mega Blade combine, they form the ultimate weapon of the Shogun: the Shogun Spear.

SHOGUN BUCKLE

The Buckle on the uniform of the Samurai Rangers has an emblem that reflects the color of each Ranger, and contains a slot in which to place Power Discs.

LIGHT ROD

The rod that the LightZord hangs from also doubles as a fighting weapon for the Gold Ranger.

SHARK SWORD

The Shark Sword comes out of a special Disc
programmed by Antonio, and has a deadly bite
that can take out whole ranks of Moogers.
When the Red Ranger uses the Shark
Sword, he goes into Shark Attack
Mode. This sword is also a Zord
and can be used by the Samurai
Megazord in Mega Mode.

ANTONIO'S MORPHER

Antonio's Morpher is unlike the others. He doesn't write his Symbol Powers like the other Rangers, but instead texts from his Morpher to summon his powers and Zords.

POWER DISCS

The Power Discs carry with them the power of Power Ranger Zords and their natural elements, and allow them to upgrade their weaponry into more powerful tools that can destroy even the most evil monsters. Special Power Discs power an arsenal of weapons the Rangers carry with them.

SAMURAI DISC

Each Ranger's black Samurai Disc powers their Spin Swords and allows them to transform their weapons into more specialized weaponry.

LION DISC

The Red Ranger's own Lion Disc attaches to his Spin Sword and powers his LionZord.

DRAGON DISC

The Blue Ranger can use his special Dragon Disc to power his Hydro Bow and his DragonZord.

APE DISC

Using her own personal Ape Disc, the Yellow Ranger can power her Earth Slicer and her ApeZord.

TURTLE DISC

The Pink Ranger's Turtle Disc powers her Sky Fan and her TurtleZord.

BEAR DISC

The Green Ranger's Bear Disc powers the Forest Spear and his BearZord.

LIGHTNING DISC

When the Lightning Disc is attached to the Red Ranger's Spin Sword, it shoots lightning bolts.

BEETLE DISC

One of the secret Discs, the Beetle Disc requires double the power of a Samurai Ranger in order to wield its power. Even the Red Ranger struggles to master it, but when he finally does, his Fire Smasher upgrades to the Five Disc Beetle Cannon. This Disc also releases and powers the BeetleZord.

CATCH DISC

By placing the Catch Disc onto a fishing pole, Kevin was able to catch the SwordfishZord. The Disc was then transformed into the lost Swordfish Disc.

SWORDFISH DISC

Recovered by Kevin after the SwordfishZord was rediscovered in the ocean, the Swordfish Disc summons and powers the SwordfishZord.

TIGER DISC

The Tiger Disc powers the TigerZord, which was lost in battle by a previous Red Ranger.

RESIST DISC

The Resist Disc has the ability to reverse powerful Nighlok spells.

CORAL DISC

The Coral Disc is the Gold Ranger's own personal Disc, which gives him the ability to text his Power Symbols.

OCTO DISC

The Octo Disc powers the Gold Ranger's OctoZord.

CLAW DISC

The Claw Disc is the Gold Ranger's double-sided Disc, and powers the ClawZord.

SUPER SAMURAI DISC

When the Super Samurai Disc is placed into the Black Box, the Samurai Rangers become Super Samurai.

SAMURAI COMBINATION DISC

When attached to the Black Box, the Samurai Combination Disc allows the Samurai Megazord to combine with the ClawZord to create the Claw Armor Megazord.

SAMURAI BATTLE DISC

The Samurai Battle Disc is the LightZord's special Disc, which shoots out like missiles from a slot inside of the Zord.

BULL DISC

The Bull Disc tames the ancient BullZord, which is released by Cody.

BULLZOOKA DISC

The Bullzooka Disc was made for the Rangers by Cody and powers the Bullzooka, a powerful laser blaster.

SHARK DISC

The Shark Disc allows the Rangers to use Shark Attack Mode and controls the SharkZord.

ULTIMATE DISC

This Ultimate Disc allows the Samurai Rangers to create the ultimate Megazord: the Samurai Gigazord.

SHOGUN DISC

The Shogun Disc allows the Rangers to access Shogun Mode.

CODY'S FATHER'S DISC

Given to Cody by his father, this was the original power Disc used by Cody's ancestors to create the BullZord. It transforms into the Bull Disc.

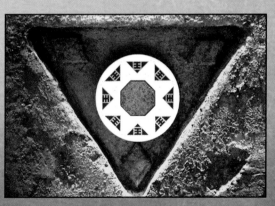

CODY'S DISC

This is the original Disc that Cody made and gave to Jayden in order to help tame the BullZord.

POWER RANGERS ZORDS

Every Samurai Ranger has in his possession a special animal Zord, which has been handed down from generation to generation. In their small FoldingZord state, these origami-like magical robots are the size of your palm and unfold into miniature Zords, but they have the ability to transform into much larger versions of themselves when the Rangers enter Mega-Mode to fight the MegaMonster versions of the Nighlok.

They are able to unfold into Zord vehicles tied to their animal spirits. When in Mega-Mode, each Zord grows into a giant vehicle driven by a Samurai Ranger. The Zords can also combine into giant Megazords, creating the ultimate giant robot fighter.

LIONZORD

The Red Ranger's Zord is the loyal and brave Lion. With lightning speed and flaming attacks, the LionZord also serves as the head and main body of the Samurai Megazord.

DRAGONZORD

The Blue Ranger's Zord is the powerful Dragon. Able to shoot blue fire at its enemies, the DragonZord combines in Mega Mode to form the Samurai Megazord's left leg.

TURTLEZORD

The Pink Ranger's Zord is the Turtle, an animal known for its tough exterior and ancient wisdom. The TurtleZord combines with the other Zords to become the right arm of the Samurai Megazord.

APEZORD

The Yellow Ranger's Zord is the strong, brave, and beastly Ape. In Mega Mode, the ApeZord becomes the left arm of the Samurai Megazord.

BEARZORD

The Green Ranger's Zord is a growling, prowling Bear always in search of Moogers and Nighlok. With claws ready to slash, the BearZord forms the right leg of the Samurai Megazord.

BEETLEZORD

One of the secret Zords passed down from previous generations of Samurai, the BeetleZord requires twice the power a Samurai typically possesses, which makes it twice as powerful.

SWORDFISHZORD

The SwordfishZord was lost long ago, but after a great struggle, Kevin managed to capture the Zord onto a Disc and bring it into their arsenal.

TIGERZORD

The TigerZord had been lost in battle against the Nighlok years ago, after which it was found and brainwashed by the evil Nighlok Madimot. The Red Ranger uses the Resist Disc to break the Zord of the spell and the TigerZord is once again the Red Ranger's loyal Zord.

OCTOZORD

As a child, the Gold Ranger was given this tentacled Zord by Jayden, his childhood friend. The OctoZord can spit a black ink to blind his opponents.

CLAWZORD

Damaged long ago in battle, the ClawZord is brought back to life by the Gold Ranger with the help of the other Rangers. As the Gold Ranger's second Zord, the ClawZord helps form the Claw Battlezord.

BULLZORD

The first Zord ever created, the BullZord ran wild and was therefore locked up for centuries. With Cody's help, the Rangers were able to tame it with a special Disc, and now it is a powerful ally.

LIGHTZORD

The LightZord was damaged in battle long ago and repaired by Antonio. It can shoot Discs out of its front compartment like missiles.

SHARKZORD

This Zord is not only a vehicle but is also used as a sword by the Samurai Megazord. The SharkZord can extend to long lengths, and literally take a bite out of the enemy.

SAMURAI MEGAZORD

When the Power Rangers need to defeat a MegaMonster Nighlok, they go into Mega Mode. The Zords they control grow extra large, and they can combine them to create super warrior robots to combat the giant Nighlok.

BEETLE BLASTER
MEGAZORD

The Beetle Blaster Megazord is created by combining
the BeetleZord and the Samurai Megazord.

SWORDFISH FENCER MEGAZORD

This Megazord is formed by combining the Samurai Megazord with the SwordfishZord. The SwordfishZord becomes both armor for the Samurai Megazord and a giant twin-bladed sword.

TIGER DRILL MEGAZORD

This Megazord is formed when the Samurai Megazord combines with the powerful TigerZord. The four drills on top are ready to dive into any opponent's defenses.

SAMURAI BATTLEWING

Formed when the TigerZord, the BeetleZord, and the SwordfishZord combine, this Megazord can fly. It attacks with the Vortex Spin and the Charging Slash.

BATTLEWING MEGAZORD

When the Blue Ranger figures out how to combine the Samurai Battlewing and Samurai Megazord, he creates the Battlewing Megazord, a Megazord that can fly and is armed with the Samurai Megazord's katana blade!

OCTO SPEAR MEGAZORD

The Gold Ranger's OctoZord combines with the Samurai Megazord to become the Octo Spear Megazord. Not only does it provide armor for the Samurai Megazord, but it also adds Spear Thrust, Ice Breath, and a Samurai Strike to the Rangers' weapon arsenal.

CLAW BATTLEZORD

In Mega Mode, the ClawZord has the ability to transform itself into the Claw Battlezord with four positions: north, south, east, and west, with each position having its own unique pattern.

CLAW ARMOR MEGAZORD

Using the power of the Black Box, the Samurai Rangers can combine the Samurai Megazord with the Claw Battlezord to create the Claw Armor Megazord.

SAMURAI BATTLE CANNON

The OctoZord combines with the Samurai Battlewing to become the Samurai Battle Cannon, which can be used as a cannon by the Claw Armor Megazord.

LIGHT MEGAZORD

When the Rangers go into Mega Mode, the LightZord can help by becoming the Light Megazord, a giant fighting robot.

SAMURAI LIGHT MEGAZORD

The Light Megazord combines with the Bear, Turtle, Ape, and DragonZords to form the Samurai Light Megazord.

SAMURAI SHARK MEGAZORD

When the Samurai Megazord calls for help from the Shark Disc, the SharkZord emerges to combine with it and become the Samurai Shark Megazord.

BULL MEGAZORD

The BullZord can turn itself into the mighty Bull Megazord, unleashing massive firepower from its shoulder cannons and a burst of Symbol Power from the Disc loaded on its head.

SAMURAI GIGAZORD

With the Ultimate Disc, the Rangers can combine all of their Zords into the mighty Samurai Gigazord.

117

POWER RANGERS
EPIC BATTLES

Though Master Xandred and his Nighlok army are on a path of destruction, we have heroes to defend us by pushing the evil back to the Netherworld. These heroes are Samurai warriors who possess mysterious powers that have been passed down from parent to child for generations. They live among us, training for the time when they will be called upon to save the world.

When Master Xandred reawakens, he sends Tooya to battle the newly formed Samurai Rangers. By having Moogers attack the city, the fire-breathing Tooya lures the Rangers into his trap. The Red Ranger relentlessly battles Tooya and strikes the Nighlok down with his Fire Smasher. When Tooya returns as a MegaMonster, the Rangers use their Zords for the first time to defeat him.

As the teens continue to learn about their new lives as Samurai Rangers, Master Xandred sends Scorpionic to terrorize Earth. Scorpionic's scythe sword, wind attack, and whipping tail cause trouble for all the Rangers, but the Red Ranger will not back down. The other Rangers work together to destroy the Nighlok and the MegaMonster by becoming the Samurai Megazord. Now the Rangers know the true power of teamwork!

Negatron is a bully who hurls insults at his victims, but these insults can hurl his victims through the air. The Samurai Rangers aren't safe, either. Only Emily is unaffected because of her past. When the Rangers finally stand up to the Nighlok, they

prove that words will never hurt them. But the Five Disc Beetle Cannon and the Beetle Blaster Megazord will destroy Negatron.

When Master Xandred sends Dayu to Earth, she proves to be a worthy opponent for the Rangers. As their swords clang, it seems that the Nighlok has the Rangers against the ropes until the Samurai Rangers use their Five Disc Cannon to launch fireballs at Dayu. Then a mysterious Nighlok named Deker swoops in to block the Rangers' attack. He warns the Red Ranger that they will eventually fight in an ultimate duel and then escapes with Dayu back into the Netherworld.

Robtish is a deadly Nighlok swordsman sent by Octoroo to destroy the Red Ranger, but Deker arrives again to drive the Nighlok back into the Netherworld. Even though Master Xandred is outraged that Deker has intervened, Deker believes that the Red Ranger is meant to be his target only and the rogue Nighlok thirsts for the ultimate duel.

Master Xandred quickly sends Robtish back to battle the Red Ranger, but this time all the Rangers are ready. Robtish is defeated by the Five Disc Tiger Cannon, but when he turns into a MegaMonster, the Blue Ranger figures out how combine the Samurai Battlewing with the Samurai Megazord to form the Battlewing Megazord, which destroys the MegaMonster with a Flying Slash finisher.

Vulpes can copy all of the Rangers' attacks with his magic mirror and can become invisible. The Rangers' Spin Swords are of no use and Vulpes's Fox Reflector uses their own Spin Sword powers against them. But then the Gold Ranger appears for the first time and takes down Vulpes with his Barracuda Blade. To battle the MegaMonster,

the Rangers form the Battlewing Megazord, but Vulpes makes himself invisible. The Rangers are in trouble until the Gold Ranger calls on the OctoZord to blast an ink cloud to reveal and demolish Vulpes.

With his Full-Body Blades attack, Steeleto goes to fight the Power Rangers to avenge Vulpes. Steeleto's slash attack nearly beats the Rangers, but the Nighlok must return to the Sanzu River when he starts to dry up. The Power Rangers prepare for his return by asking the Gold Ranger to join their team. When Steeleto attacks again, the Nighlok

is defeated by the Red and Gold Rangers' Barracuda Bite and Blazing Strike finishers. But MegaMonster Steeleto's Full-Body Blades attack and weaken the Samurai Megazord until the Gold Ranger summons the

OctoZord. The OctoZord and Samurai Megazord combine to form the Octo Spear Megazord to zap Steeleto with its Electric Spear attack.

Splitface is hungry for one thing and one thing only: human souls! When the Rangers confront the Nighlok, Splitface steals the Yellow Ranger's soul and escapes back to the Netherworld, promising never to return. To save the Yellow Ranger, the other Rangers combine their Symbol Power and drag Splitface back into their world. The Rangers instantly destroy the surprised Nighlok, but this MegaMonster wants to fight! The Gold Ranger turns the ClawZord into the powerful Claw Battlezord East, Claw Battlezord West, and Claw Battlezord South to annihilate the giant Nighlok and free all of the human souls the beast had trapped, including the Yellow Ranger's.

The Mutant Arachnitor is wreaking havoc throughout the city, but the Nighlok is too strong for the Rangers. Before the Nighlok can attack again, Antonio finishes the Black Box that allows the Red Ranger to combine all of the Samurai Rangers' powers so that he can morph into the Super Samurai Red Ranger. Now a force to reckon with, the Super Samurai Red Ranger overpowers the Mutant Arachnitor and the Moogers. And when the MegaMonster rises, the

Rangers call out their Super Samurai combination and form the Claw Armor Megazord, blasting the Nighlok with their Samurai Battle Cannon.

Master Xandred sends Armadeevil to the human world to battle the Samurai Rangers with his indestructible shell. While the Rangers struggle at first, they follow Kevin's plan to hit Armadeevil with a series of attacks that heat his shell, then quickly cool it, making it brittle. Then the Blue Ranger uses the Black Box to defeat Armadeevil with a powerful blow to his shell.

In the Netherworld, Serrator, a mysterious and powerful Nighlok, convinces Master Xandred to allow him to go to the human world and help flood the earth. Serrator proves to be very strong, and the Rangers are shaken when his paper-doll army of Papyrux attack. The Samurai Rangers struggle in their battles, but before they can be defeated, the Gold Ranger arrives with the LightZord and attacks Serrator. The sly Nighlok admits that he underestimated the Rangers and escapes back through a gap, biding his time until he can strike again.

Octoroo, with the help of the Nighlok Eyescar, kidnaps Antonio and Mentor Ji to use as bait in order to lead the rest of the Rangers into

a Mooger trap. The Rangers fight a losing battle until the Green Ranger grabs the Light-Zord and fires the mysterious Disc that Antonio was working on. The Shark Disc allows the Red Ranger and his sword to morph into Shark Attack Mode and the powerful Shark Sword. With the power of the new Disc, he quickly defeats the Moogers, ambushes Eyescar, and frees Antonio and Ji.

When the evil Skarf is let loose on the city, the team must scramble to stop him. Deker and Dayu show up and join in the fight against them, until they turn on the Nighlok and strike Skarf down! Skarf rises up as a MegaMonster, more powerful than ever, revealing that Dayu and Deker have unlocked his power. As a last-ditch effort, the Mega Blue Ranger convinces the team to try a dangerous combination of new Discs that form the Samurai Gigazord, with which they are able to finally defeat Skarf.

When Serrator refuses to give back Dayu's Harmonium to help soothe him, Master Xandred follows Serrator to the human world! When the Rangers are alerted that there are Moogers to destroy, they walk into the middle of Serrator and Master Xandred's epic battle. Once Serrator escapes, Master Xandred turns his furious attention to the Red Ranger and they finally fight head-to-head. Master Xandred defeats the Red Ranger soundly, but before he can deliver the final blow, Xandred dries out from a lack of Sanzu River water and must return to the Netherworld. Octoroo turns his Giant Moogers on the remaining Rangers, but the MegaMonsters are easily destroyed by the Bull Megazord and Claw Armor Megazord. Meanwhile, Master Xandred and Jayden are wounded, but both will heal in time to fight another day.